Marching in Birmingham

MARCHING IN
BIRMINGHAM

William J. Boerst

MORGAN
REYNOLDS
PUBLISHING

Greensboro, North Carolina

THE CIVIL RIGHTS MOVEMENT

The Trial of the Scottsboro Boys

Marching in Birmingham

Selma and the Voting Rights Act

The Murder of Emmett Till

Freedom Summer

MARCHING IN BIRMINGHAM

Copyright © 2008 by William J. Boerst

Library of Congress Cataloging-in-Publication Data

Boerst, William J.
    Marching in Birmingham / by William J. Boerst.
        p. cm. -- (Civil rights series)
    Includes bibliographical references and index.
    ISBN-13: 978-1-59935-055-4
    ISBN-10: 1-59935-055-6
    1. African Americans--Civil rights--Alabama--Birmingham--History--20th
century--Juvenile literature. 2. Civil rights movements--Alabama--Birmingham-
-History--20th century--Juvenile literature. 3. African American civil rights
workers--Alabama--Birmingham--History--20th century--Juvenile literature. 4.
King, Martin Luther, Jr., 1929-1968--Juvenile literature. 5. Birmingham (Ala.)-
-Race relations--History--20th century--Juvenile literature. I. Title.
    F334.B69N426 2008
    323.1196'0730761781--dc22
                                                    2007026640

Printed in the United States of America
First Edition

For Fran Taft, Wayne Anderson, and Dmitri Italiano

Contents

Ralph Abernathy (left) and Martin Luther King Jr. lead a group of demonstrators as they march toward the city hall in Birmingham. *(Courtesy of AP Images/Horace Cort)*

one
Birmingham Jail

On the morning of April 12, 1963, Martin Luther King Jr., Fred Shuttlesworth, and other leaders of the civil rights movement sat in a hotel room in Birmingham, Alabama, and planned their next move. Shuttlesworth was a minister at a local church, and he had been protesting the city's strict enforcement of racial segregation for years. King and his civil rights organization, the Southern Christian Leadership Conference (SCLC), had arrived in town two weeks earlier to help Shuttlesworth lead a campaign of marches and sit-ins that they hoped would end segregation in the city. Success in Birmingham would be a major victory for the civil rights movement, but so far it was not going well.

Small protests and sit-ins had led to a number of arrests, but the city's restaurants, restrooms, bus stations, and other facilities remained segregated. The SCLC was running out of money to bail protestors out of jail, and the Birmingham court had just issued an injunction temporarily prohibiting any further demonstrations. Anyone who took part in a protest would immediately be arrested. King had planned to lead a march on the afternoon of the twelfth, but if he did he would go to jail at a time when the campaign badly needed money. If he postponed the march, he could travel to the North to try to raise more money, but he worried that the campaign might lose what little momentum it had while he was gone.

To make matters worse, the SCLC had been defeated in an earlier attempt to end segregation in Albany, Georgia. If King and the SCLC lost another battle, the entire civil rights movement might come to a halt. Something dramatic was needed for the Birmingham campaign to recover. After discussing the situation with his friends and advisors in the hotel, King went into another room to think and pray. When he returned, he had changed into a work shirt and blue jeans—he was ready to go to jail. That afternoon, King and Ralph Abernathy, the treasurer of the SCLC, led a group of about fifty marchers toward city hall. Police soon arrested most of the protestors, and King and Abernathy were placed in solitary confinement.

King had little contact with others during his eight days in jail, but he used his time productively. After reading a letter written by a number of local white religious leaders urging the black community to stop the protests, King began writing a reply. Using the margins of newspaper and other scraps of paper, King composed a long letter outlining the reasons for the demonstrations.

King described the extent of racism in Birmingham and argued that nothing would change unless he and other African

Downtown Birmingham in 1963 *(Courtesy of AP Images)*

Americans demanded their rights. "Birmingham is probably the most thoroughly segregated city in the United States," he wrote. "Its ugly record of brutality is widely known." Birmingham's white community had often used violence to enforce segregation. One black neighborhood had even been nicknamed "Dynamite Hill" because bombings of homes owned by African Americans there were so common.

Although King agreed with the white religious leaders that the protests were unfortunate, he blamed the white community for its unequal treatment of African Americans: "We had no alternative except to prepare for direct action." The nonviolent tactics the protestors used, he said, were intended to create a "crisis" that would force local white officials to negotiate and, hopefully, to give African Americans the rights they deserved. King conceded that he had broken the law by protesting despite the court's injunction, but he called it an unjust law. And, he said, he had a "moral responsibility to disobey unjust laws."

Many white residents argued that if African Americans were just more patient they would eventually be given their rights, but King responded to this as well:

> For years now I have heard the words 'Wait!' It rings in the ear of every Negro with a piercing familiarity. The 'Wait' has almost always meant 'Never.. . . Let us all hope that the dark clouds of racial prejudice will soon pass away and the deep fog of misunderstanding will be lifted from our fear-drenched communities, and in some not too distant tomorrow the radiant stars of love and brotherhood will shine over our great nation with all their scintillating beauty.

King and Abernathy were released on bond after eight days in jail. The long letter was soon published and eventually became famous for its statement of the justification for nonviolent protests. Of course, if the Birmingham campaign had failed, the letter might never have attracted much attention. But other protestors had continued to demonstrate while the two leaders were in jail, and popular singer Harry Belafonte had helped raise money for the campaign in the North. The movement was a long way from victory, but it had at least been saved from failure.

In early May, there was finally a breakthrough. The primary problem up to this point had been a lack of demonstrators; not enough members of the black community were willing to go to jail. King's promise to fill the jails of Birmingham looked like an empty threat. But another experienced civil rights activist, James Bevel, urged King to enlist high school and even elementary school students in the movement.

Beginning on May 2, hundreds of young African Americans skipped school to take part in massive protests. Over the next few days, their efforts were met with violence by local police and firemen, who used fire hoses and police dogs to try to discourage the demonstrators. Pictures of young black men and women being blasted with water from powerful hoses and bitten by dogs made front-page news across the country.

Birmingham's white community criticized King, Shuttlesworth, and the other civil rights leaders for allowing such young students to take part in dangerous demonstrations, and parents of some of the students were upset as well. But Birmingham's long history of racism and segregation convinced the black leaders that there was no other choice. If the campaign for racial equality was going to succeed in Birmingham, it would be because of the willingness of these students to demand their rights.

two
The Magic City

I n Alabama, as in the rest of the South, segregation had long been a part of everyday life. In the years following the end of the Civil War in 1865, Congress had tried to help African Americans gain more political and civil rights. A series of constitutional amendments improved life for freed slaves but did not end discrimination. The Thirteenth Amendment, passed in 1865, outlawed slavery. Three years later, the Fourteenth Amendment made African Americans full citizens, and in 1870 the Fifteenth Amendment gave black men the right to vote. But at the same time, southern states began to pass laws known as "Black Codes" to try to take away the new rights of African Americans.

State governments in the South also created rules that made it almost impossible for blacks to register to vote. Some states rewrote their constitutions to add qualifications such as literacy tests and poll taxes for those who tried to register. Even if a black man was able to register, he would face the

A poster illustrates the rights granted by the Fifteenth Amendment. Although a series of constitutional amendments improved life for freed slaves after 1865, Southern states began to pass laws that limited the rights of African Americans. *(Library of Congress)*

threat of violence and even death if he actually went to cast a ballot. This type of violence against African Americans was rarely punished. White policemen would usually not make arrests in these cases, and those whites that did go to trial for crimes against African Americans would almost certainly be found not guilty by all-white juries.

By the end of the nineteenth century, segregation was firmly entrenched throughout the South. This system of ensuring white power became known as Jim Crow, named after a character from minstrel shows, a popular form of

The Supreme Court's decision in *Plessy v. Ferguson* reinforced the practice of racial segregation, making it legal to have separate public facilities for blacks and whites. (*Library of Congress*)

entertainment in the nineteenth century. The United States Supreme Court reinforced the legality of segregation in the 1896 case *Plessy v. Ferguson*. The case involved a challenge to segregated railroad cars in Louisiana. The court ruled that states could have separate facilities for blacks and whites as long as the facilities were equal. In the South, however, the facilities designated for blacks were rarely equal. African Americans had little choice but to try to live within these rules. Even the slightest show of disrespect toward a white person could potentially end violently.

Birmingham was not founded until 1871, six years after the end of the Civil War, but it was no exception in its enforcement of segregation. It quickly became an industrial center with an economy dominated by the iron, steel, and manufacturing industries. Its rapid growth led to the nickname "The Magic City."

Local politics were run by a group of men known as the "Big Mules." These men owned and ran the industries that drove the local economy. The Big Mules only hired African Americans for the lowest-paying jobs in their companies, reserving the better jobs for whites. They strongly supported Jim Crow laws. Almost all of the city's white workers also opposed any changes to the city's system of segregation.

The white community's support of segregation was maintained by an all-white police force led by Public Safety Commissioner Eugene "Bull" Connor. Connor was virtually an institution in Birmingham, having served as commissioner of public safety since 1937 (other than a brief hiatus in the mid-1950s). Connor had the support of the Big Mules because he had always opposed allowing workers to unionize, and he had the support of the white working class because of his willingness to use violence to enforce segregation.

By the early 1960s, a growing civil rights movement was fighting against segregation and discrimination. Although opposing segregation was difficult and dangerous, some African Americans had been fighting against Jim Crow laws for decades. In 1909, a small group of white and black activists in the North created the National Association for the Advancement of Colored People (NAACP). The NAACP used the law to fight racism, often defending blacks falsely accused of crimes.

In 1954, the NAACP won a major legal victory against segregation. It argued that the tradition of having "separate but equal" facilities for blacks and whites was unconstitutional. In the case *Brown v. Board of Education of Topeka,*

Rosa Parks is fingerprinted after being arrested for refusing to give up her seat to a white man on a segregated bus. *(Library of Congress)*

Kansas, the Supreme Court ruled in favor of the NAACP, finding that the facilities were rarely equal. White southerners were outraged by the Brown decision and fought to maintain segregation, so at first little changed. But the ruling gave African Americans an opening to challenge Jim Crow.

In 1955, African Americans in Montgomery, Alabama, began a campaign that would become another milestone in the civil rights movement. On December 1, an African American woman, Rosa Parks, refused to give up her seat to a white man on a segregated bus. After she was arrested, Montgomery's black community began a boycott of the buses that lasted more than a year, ending only after a ruling by the Supreme Court that declared segregation on city buses unconstitutional. The Montgomery bus boycott also marked the beginning of Martin Luther King's career as a civil rights activist. He was elected to lead the movement in Montgomery and soon after formed the Southern Christian Leadership Conference to fight discrimination elsewhere in the South.

Inspired by the Brown decision, some African Americans began trying to integrate schools. Despite the ruling, most southern school districts remained segregated, and the federal government had not yet intervened to force schools to integrate.

On September 23, 1957, black students attempted to attend classes at a white high school in Little Rock, Arkansas, but they were forced to flee by an angry white mob. President Dwight D. Eisenhower sent army troops to the city to enforce integration. Two days later, the soldiers surrounded the high school and escorted the nine students into the school.

Eisenhower was not a strong supporter of civil rights, but he did believe that the law had to be upheld, and he was angry that Arkansas officials were too stubborn to allow integration without federal intervention. Even after desegregation in Little Rock, however, most other southern cities continued to maintain segregated schools. African Americans would have to make progress one city at a time.

In 1960, African American college students began using another tactic to fight segregation. On February 1, 1960, four black students in Greensboro, North Carolina, sat at a segregated lunch counter at a local Woolworth's department store and asked to be served. They were denied service but remained at the counter in protest. The next day, they returned

College students stage a sit-in at a lunch counter in Nashville. *(Library of Congress)*

with more students. By the third day, black students took up almost all of the lunch counter's seats. Within five days, hundreds of college students were part of sit-ins at various lunch counters in Greensboro.

Sit-ins were dangerous, though. Many protestors were insulted, arrested, or even beaten, and there was little hope that the federal government would protect them. However, this wasn't enough to deter the protestors.

By the end of the year, as many as 70,000 students across the South had taken part in the sit-in movement. The sit-ins relied on a different strategy than the civil rights movement had used before. The students themselves were the actual protest, not lawsuits or boycotts. Sit-ins forced whites to notice and to decide how to react. As the sit-in movement spread across the South, it was clear that things were changing.

Arthur "A. G." Gaston *(Library of Congress)*

In Birmingham, however, change was slow to arrive. One problem, of course, was the white community's widespread support for segregation. Another problem was that the black community was divided. Some African Americans had been able to achieve economic success despite the many obstacles. Arthur "A. G." Gaston, for example, had become quite wealthy. He got his start in business by selling insurance to African Americans, then expanded into other businesses. Eventually he ran funeral homes, a hotel, and a bank. Gaston rarely challenged white leaders of the city on civil rights issues, preferring to focus on the business ventures that had made him so successful. The city's other black professionals—the doctors, lawyers, ministers, and teachers—also tended to avoid civil rights issues because it would put their tenuous success at risk.

Birmingham's black community also had little political power because few African Americans had been able to register to vote. By 1960, the city's population was more than 340,000. About 135,000 of the residents were black, 40 percent of the population. But less than 10 percent of the black community was registered to vote. Birmingham's growing black population also meant that more houses needed to be built in black neighborhoods, but the city maintained zoning codes that determined where blacks and whites could live, creating a housing shortage.

The lack of adequate housing for African Americans soon became a major source of racial tension. A 1926 zoning ordinance limited African Americans to certain areas of the city. Some African Americans tried to move into houses near white neighborhoods, but they were met with fierce opposition. In 1946, an African American named Sam Matthews bought a lot close to a white neighborhood. He went to court to sue for the right to occupy the lot and won the case, but on August 18, 1947, white vigilantes threw six sticks of dynamite into the house and destroyed it.

In 1948, a black couple, Johnnie and Emily Madison, bought a house formerly owned by whites. After being assured that there would not be a problem with living there, they began redecorating the home in 1949. But one night, around

Between 1947 and 1965 more than fifty African American houses were bombed in Birmingham. Passersby stop to observe a house that has been bombed. *(Library of Congress)*

midnight, the home was destroyed by a dynamite blast. Two other houses on the street met the same fate.

Between 1947 and 1965 there were more than fifty similar bombings of houses occupied by blacks in Birmingham. In 1949, the city created an ordinance that made it a misdemeanor for a black person to move into a white neighborhood. The author of the ordinance, James Simpson, explained that if blacks were allowed to move into white neighborhoods, it would lead to "disorders and bloodshed and our ancient and excellent plan of life here in Alabama is gone." The local black newspaper, the *Birmingham World*, complained that "Negro citizens are bottled in the slums and restricted to the blighted areas."

The threat of violence made it dangerous for African Americans in Birmingham to protest against bombings.

But there were some African Americans who disregarded their own safety and began agitating for civil rights long before Martin Luther King arrived in 1963. And no one did more to fight segregation and discrimination in Birmingham than Fred Shuttlesworth.

Shuttlesworth gained national recognition in 1963 for working with King and the SCLC, but he had been well

Fred Shuttlesworth (*Library of Congress*)

known in Birmingham for years. He was born March 18, 1922, near Montgomery, Alabama, and moved with his mother to Birmingham when he was three. As a child, he sold newspapers and used the money he earned to buy a bicycle. He did well in school and admired his teachers. Later, he wrote of his teachers, "I believed in them and they believed in me. These were the people from whom I learned to analyze things." He was valedictorian of his high school class in 1940 and soon took a job as a handyman in a doctor's office. While working there he met a nursing student, Ruby Keeler. They were married in October 1941. Two years later, in the middle of World War II, the couple moved to Mobile, Alabama, when Shuttlesworth took a job at a nearby Air Force base.

As much as he admired teachers, Shuttlesworth's heroes were ministers. He said of one of them, "I would rather hear Mr. Hawthorne pray than to eat; I always wanted to pray like that." One night he attended a Baptist church service and was moved by the energy there. He joined the church and began to feel that God wanted him to preach. He received a preaching license from a Baptist church. When he was not busy at work, he would study the Bible. He also started taking classes at a local seminary, and then began attending Selma College. He taught public school while working toward his degree and eventually earned degrees from both Selma College and Alabama State College.

Shuttlesworth was soon hired by the First Baptist Church of Selma, in Selma, Alabama. But he was very strong willed, and he tended to see issues in absolutes, making him difficult to work with. He clashed with the deacons of the church, leading to his resignation in December 1952. In the spring of 1953, he took a position with Bethel Baptist Church in Birmingham, returning to the city where he had grown up.

When the Supreme Court handed down their decision in *Brown v. Board of Education*, it had little effect in Birmingham. Shuttlesworth, however, realized the importance of the decision and began to take a more active role in fighting for civil rights. He was a member of the Baptist Ministers' Conference, a group of local black ministers. Shuttlesworth suggested the idea of trying to get black policemen hired, but the Conference refused to take part in such a campaign. So Shuttlesworth met with many of the members of the Conference individually and convinced seventy-seven of them to sign a petition calling for the hiring of black policemen. They presented the petition to the city commissioners, who said that they could not act because it would anger the white community.

The local branch of the NAACP recognized Shuttlesworth's tenacity and leadership ability and named him membership chairman. As chairman, Shuttlesworth tried to get local black leaders more involved in protesting segregation, but in 1956 a state court outlawed the NAACP in Alabama. The state government hoped that by making it illegal to be a member of the NAACP they could prevent any further efforts against white supremacy.

Shuttlesworth and several other ministers in Birmingham responded by deciding to form a new civil rights organization. The ministers held a large gathering at a local Baptist church on June 5, 1956. The night before, they had met to discuss the purpose of the new group, which they had named the Alabama Christian Movement for Human Rights (ACMHR). More than one thousand people attended the mass meeting. The crowd approved the goals agreed on by Shuttlesworth and the other founders, despite the opposition of some members of the Baptists Ministers' Conference. Birmingham's traditional black leaders, including economic leaders like Gaston and many of the city's black ministers, opposed the formation of the new organization, perhaps because they were afraid it would take away some of their power. Few members of the black upper class joined the ACMHR, so the organization's membership consisted largely of lower middle-class black residents. The primary goals of the ACMHR were to provide the black community with the same opportunity as whites for economic and social advancement.

Shuttlesworth and other African Americans sit among whites on this Birmingham bus to protest segregation. *(Library of Congress)*

Shuttlesworth and the ACMHR quickly went to work to try to reach those lofty goals. One of their first actions was to start a bus boycott modeled on the successful boycott in Montgomery. After the Supreme Court ruled in November 1956 that segregated seating was unconstitutional, Shuttlesworth wrote letters to the city government asking them to integrate the city's buses, but the city refused. On Christmas Eve, the ACMHR held a meeting to discuss the boycott. About 1,500 African Americans listened as Shuttlesworth told them how to use nonviolent tactics to integrate the buses. The next night, Christmas, Shuttlesworth sat in his house talking with one of the church deacons. Outside, white supremacists drove by and threw six sticks of dynamite under the house. The bomb went off, throwing Shuttlesworth into the air. Somehow, he escaped unharmed. The deacon and two of Shuttlesworth's children were injured, but not seriously.

Despite this kind of opposition, Shuttlesworth led about 250 members of the ACMHR onto local buses the next morning. They sat in the white section of the buses, and although there was no violence, twenty-one were eventually arrested. The case against the protestors slowly made its way through the courts. Judges in local and state courts rarely supported civil rights for African Americans, so the ACMHR had to keep appealing rulings against them until the case reached a federal court, which took until the fall of 1958. Birmingham's white leaders knew that they would lose, so instead of continuing with the case they created a new law that gave the private bus company the right to determine where riders should sit.

Now Shuttlesworth and the ACMHR had to start all over. In October, they again rode the buses and sat in the white sections. This time, thirteen riders were arrested. Not until December 1959 did this case make its way to federal court, where a judge found in favor of the ACMHR. After years of effort, the city's buses were desegregated. But the opposition of the city's white leaders to even this small protest showed how far they were willing to go to maintain Jim Crow.

Shuttlesworth launched other attacks on segregation as well. In 1957, he tried to register four children, including two of his own, at a white school. A white mob, aware of what Shuttlesworth was planning to do, attacked the small group, beating them with clubs, brass knuckles, and bicycle chains. Shuttlesworth and the students escaped with their lives.

Birmingham could not remain isolated forever from the changes sweeping across the South. In 1961, buses carrying groups of black and white protestors brought the national civil rights movement, and the eyes of the country, to Birmingham.

three

The Freedom Rides Come to Birmingham

In the spring of 1961, black and white members of the Congress of Racial Equality (CORE), a civil rights organization, decided to travel together from Washington, D.C., to New Orleans by bus. The Supreme Court had ruled in 1960 that segregation in bus stations was unconstitutional, but southern states had not yet integrated their facilities. Bus stations in the South still had "white" and "black" sitting areas, restrooms, and even water fountains, and seating on the buses was still segregated. The members of CORE knew that white southerners might react violently to interracial groups of travelers, but they hoped that the federal government would intervene to protect their rights. After all, the protestors had the law on their side; in this case, at least, it was segregation that was illegal.

Thirteen protestors—Freedom Riders as they became known—boarded two buses in Washington on May 4. Some white riders sat in the back of the bus, most of the black riders

A segregated bus station prominently displays a "White Waiting Room" sign. *(Library of Congress)*

sat in the front, and some sat together. The first two days of the trip went smoothly, with some rude stares but no violence. But on the third day, after the first bus pulled into Rock Hill, South Carolina, a group of white men confronted the riders. John Lewis, a young leader of the civil rights movement and later a member of Congress, was the first to be attacked. He and one other black rider were beaten until police intervened and stopped the assault. For the next few days, however, the rides again went well, and the buses reached Atlanta on Saturday, May 13. There, the riders met with Martin Luther King and prepared to head to Alabama.

The next morning, Mother's Day, the two buses left Atlanta and headed for Birmingham. The first bus, a Greyhound, left slightly earlier and was scheduled to arrive

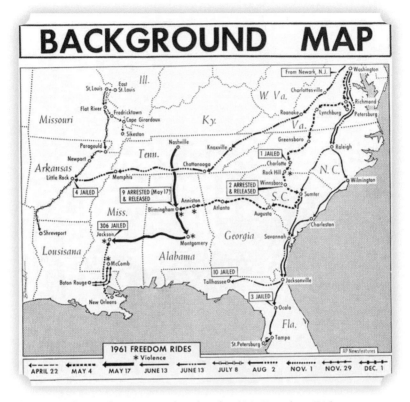

This map shows the routes taken by the 1961 Freedom Riders. *(Courtesy of AP Images)*

in the afternoon at 3:30. The second bus, a Trailways, was scheduled to arrive at four. For the first bus, the trouble began soon after crossing the state line and entering Alabama. It pulled into Anniston, a small city of 30,000 about sixty miles east of Birmingham, in mid-afternoon and was met at the bus station by an angry mob of white men. The mob tried to force its way onto the bus, but two state policemen who were traveling on the bus in plain clothes barred the door shut. Realizing that it was too dangerous to try to make this scheduled stop, the driver pulled back out and headed down the highway toward Birmingham, but not before the tires had

Protesters display signs during a Freedom Ride. *(Library of Congress)*

been slashed. A long line of cars pursued the bus, which had to pull over when the tires went flat.

The pursuing mob broke the bus windows and threw a firebomb into the bus, forcing the riders to try to escape the smoking wreck. The whites who surrounded the bus might have killed at least some of the riders, but one of the policemen on the bus waved his gun to try to scare the attackers away. Although none of the riders were killed, several were badly beaten, and all were deeply frightened. More state police finally arrived and took the passengers to a hospital in Anniston.

Riders on the second bus did not hear about what had happened until they arrived in Anniston. They got off the bus and some bought food, but as they returned to their seats a group of white men boarded the bus and began beating the riders. They first attacked a college freshman. When two white riders came forward to help him, they were pummeled to the floor. The attackers dragged the beaten riders to the back of the bus and then sat down for the ride to Birmingham.

Freedom Riders sit on the ground after their bus was firebombed just outside of Anniston, Alabama. *(Library of Congress)*

Bull Connor knew that the Freedom Riders were scheduled to arrive in Birmingham that afternoon, but he was not about to provide them with the protection of the local police department. Instead, he made sure that local members of the Ku Klux Klan, a large white supremacist organization, would meet the buses at the Birmingham terminals, and he arranged to give them fifteen minutes to attack the riders before the police would arrive. Connor had close ties to local leaders of the Ku Klux Klan, which meant that bombings or other attacks on the black community by the Klan were rarely investigated.

A group of thirty or forty white men waited all afternoon at the Greyhound station for the first bus to arrive. When they heard that the bus had been bombed outside Anniston, they quickly hurried several blocks down the street to the Trailways station to welcome the second bus. As the Freedom Riders stepped off the bus, already bloodied from the attacks in Anniston, they were met by dozens of angry white men. The confrontation quickly turned into a riot, as the white mob began attacking the riders. A reporter for *CBS* described the beating of one of the riders: "One passenger was knocked down at my feet by twelve of the hoodlums and his face was beaten and kicked until it was a bloody pulp." The reporter added that the terminal was not far from the police station, yet the police did not arrive until the riders had been badly injured. A number of reporters and bystanders were also attacked. The next day, pictures and stories of the violence made front-page news across the country.

Back in Anniston, the hospitalized riders were not yet safe. They had been followed even to the hospital, and were asked to leave by the hospital staff to avoid violence. To prevent further attacks, Fred Shuttlesworth helped organize a caravan to drive to Anniston to rescue the Freedom Riders.

Everyone had survived so far, but the future of the mission was in doubt. After a meeting the next day, May 15, at Shuttlesworth's house, the riders decided to try to keep going. That afternoon, they went to the bus station but found that none of the drivers were willing to drive a bus with Freedom Riders on it. Finally, after hours of waiting, the exhausted activists decided to fly to New Orleans so that they could get there in time to participate in a mass civil rights rally.

It appeared that the Freedom Rides had come to an end. But Diane Nash, a student civil rights activist in Nashville, Tennessee, saw the flight to New Orleans as an act of surrender to segregation and violence. She was a member of the Student Nonviolent Coordinating Committee (SNCC), which had formed in 1960 during the student sit-in movement and had grown quickly. Nash decided that some local members of SNCC in Nashville should continue the Freedom Rides. She called Shuttlesworth and told him her plans. He tried to discourage her, saying that the previous riders had almost been killed, but she would not change her mind. On Wednesday, May 17, ten determined students, eight black and two white, left for Birmingham. Nash stayed behind in Nashville to monitor the riders' progress.

The Birmingham police had found out about the plans, and they met the bus carrying the riders before it even reached the station. They held the new riders at the terminal for hours until Bull Connor arrived and had them all arrested. It was for their own safety, said Connor. Late that night, Connor had seven of the activists put into unmarked police cars, and he then took the riders back to Tennessee. (One of the riders had been picked up by her father, and two others had already been released.) Just after crossing over the state line, Connor had the cars stop, and he told the riders to get out. He left them along the side of the road, about halfway between Birmingham and Nashville.

After the riders were able to convince an African American couple that lived nearby to feed them, Diane Nash sent a car to return the riders to Birmingham. They were not yet ready to give up. Nash had already sent eleven more volunteers to Birmingham after the first group was arrested. By that afternoon, eighteen young activists were gathered at Shuttlesworth's house discussing what to do next. Eventually they headed to the bus station, where they hoped to take a bus scheduled to leave for Montgomery, Alabama, at five o'clock. The bus, however, would not leave on time. The bus company could not find anyone willing to drive to Montgomery with the Freedom Riders on board. The protestors spent the night in the terminal, singing and talking.

Meanwhile, the attacks in Anniston and Birmingham had forced the federal government to take an active role to prevent further violence. Protecting students riding buses was not how President John F. Kennedy had hoped he would spend his presidency, but he was compelled to respond to the trouble in Alabama. Kennedy had an ambitious foreign policy agenda, but racial violence was threatening to overshadow all other issues.

Since the end of World War II in 1945, the United States and the Soviet Union had grown increasingly wary of each other. The Cold War, as the confrontation between the two countries was known, pitted the democratic United States against the Communist Soviet Union. An important part of the Cold War was public relations. Both countries were trying to convince smaller countries around the world to become their allies. In this battle for public opinion, racism in the South had serious consequences for American foreign policy. President Kennedy knew that stories about segregation and violence made the United States look bad to the rest of the world and made his job more difficult.

At the same time, Kennedy did not want to lose the votes of white Southerners. If he supported the Freedom Riders too strongly and too openly, he was likely to cede political support in the South. For much of his administration, Kennedy tried to walk a tightrope that would allow him to appease both sides so that he could remain focused on what he believed to be more important foreign policy issues. So as the Freedom Rides developed, President Kennedy and his brother, Attorney General Robert Kennedy, worked to try to resolve the crisis peacefully without having to send in federal troops to protect the riders. The Kennedys sent an aide, John Siegenthaler, to speak with Alabama governor John Patterson. To the relief of the president, the governor promised to protect the riders.

Finally, early in the morning on Saturday, May 20, a bus driver agreed to take the riders to Montgomery. Surrounded by police cars and watched by a police helicopter, the bus left Birmingham and made its way to Alabama's capital. As the bus approached Montgomery, the helicopter and state police cars pulled away. Once the bus reached the city limits, it should have been met by city police. Instead, the Freedom Riders were welcomed by an angry mob. White men and women alike beat the riders with pipes, sticks, and bats. They smashed news cameras and attacked cameramen. Several of the riders were beaten nearly to death. Siegenthaler arrived and tried to help two of the riders, but he was seized by the mob, beaten, and left for dead. After ten or fifteen minutes of brutal assaults, police began arriving and clearing the area. Even when the mob had left, however, the police refused to take the battered Freedom Riders to the hospital. They had to wait for a black ambulance to make its way to the terminal before they received treatment.

News of the violence quickly spread across the country. Martin Luther King arrived that afternoon to speak at a rally, as did Fred Shuttlesworth. More than one thousand African Americans gathered in a black Baptist church that

Protected by state troopers and National Guardsmen, these Freedom Riders board a bus as they prepare to leave Birmingham. *(Library of Congress)*

night. Outside, another mob of Klansmen surrounded the church and began throwing rocks. They were held back only by the presence of federal marshals and, later in the night, the Alabama National Guard. The African Americans in the church were trapped there all night by the mob, unable to leave until early the next morning. In their speeches to the large gathering, King and Shuttlesworth criticized Governor Patterson for his inaction and blamed him for the violence.

On Wednesday morning, after a few days of rest, twelve of the Freedom Riders continued their journey accompanied by reporters and members of the National Guard. Over the rest of the summer, hundreds more protestors would take part in other Freedom Rides. Many of them were arrested, but there were no more scenes as violent as those in Alabama. The riders had forced the federal government to intervene, winning an important victory for the civil rights movement.

four

A City Divided

The Freedom Ride riots even made news in Japan. Birmingham businessman Sidney Smyer heard about the Freedom Ride riots while in Tokyo on business. Smyer was part of a group of Birmingham business leaders trying to encourage foreign investment in their city. But when Japanese papers carried pictures of the white mob attacking the young protestors, Smyer found it difficult to explain to his hosts why his fellow white residents of Birmingham would react so violently to people riding a bus.

This experience convinced Smyer that Birmingham had to change. The negative attention that resulted from the riots was very bad for business. After returning from abroad, Smyer began working on a plan to improve race relations and even end segregation in Birmingham.

Smyer was not the only white member of the community who was disgusted by the violence. Other local professionals—small business owners, lawyers, and others

Bull Connor *(Courtesy of AP Images)*

involved in the growing service economy that now rivaled manufacturing as the city's economic base—agreed that something had to be done, even if they still supported segregation. Many blamed Bull Connor for allowing the attacks to occur. Connor, however, still had many supporters, including the Big Mules. The clash within Birmingham's white community pitted the leaders of the old steel and iron industries against more moderate businessmen like Smyer who believed that the city had to change if it was going to continue to grow.

Despite the controversy surrounding the Freedom Ride riots, Connor continued to do everything in his power to maintain segregation. When a judge ruled on October 24, 1961, that Birmingham had to desegregate its many parks, playgrounds, and swimming pools, Connor and the other city commissioners simply closed all of them. Some of Birmingham's white residents were angered by this decision, including Smyer and his allies. They decided to take drastic measures—they would try to change the city's form of government and throw Connor out of office.

Birmingham was governed by a three-person city commission. In 1961, the commissioners were Connor, J. T. Waggoner, and Art Hanes, the mayor. Like Connor, both Waggoner and

Hanes were strong supporters of segregation. Elections had just been held earlier that year, and the terms were scheduled to run until 1965. Not wanting to wait that long for change, Smyer's group of racial moderates came up with a plan to hold a public referendum to vote on changing the city's government. Instead of a three-person commission, they wanted to create a ten-person city council led by a mayor.

After Smyer and his allies collected signatures to force a vote on changing the city government, the referendum was scheduled for November 6, 1962. The racial moderates had the local media and the black community on their side. African Americans were skeptical that a new form of government would actually change anything, but it had to be better than having Bull Connor in charge. Connor attacked Smyer and the other businessmen, calling them communists and integrationists.

When the votes had been counted, the racial moderates had won. Birmingham would have a new form of city government. New elections were scheduled for March. Connor declared that he would now run for mayor. Running against him would be Albert Boutwell, a local lawyer who had the support of the business community. He was a strong supporter of segregation, but he disapproved of the violent and very public tactics used by Connor to enforce it. Several other candidates announced that they would run as well, but Boutwell and Connor had the most backing.

On March 5, 1963, Connor and Boutwell won more votes than any other candidates, but neither gained the required 50 percent of the total votes. To decide who would be the next mayor, a runoff election between the two candidates was scheduled for April 2. When that day arrived, Birmingham

King's eloquent speeches made him a famous figure in the civil rights movement. *(Library of Congress)*

voted for change, electing Boutwell with 29,630 votes to Connor's 21,648. Connor and the other two city commissioners, however, refused to leave office. They claimed that the November referendum had been illegal and appealed the elections in court. By April 15, when Boutwell and the new city council took office, the case had still not been decided. Birmingham now had two governments.

While Birmingham's white community debated about how their city should be governed, Fred Shuttlesworth, Martin Luther King Jr., and other civil rights leaders planned a major assault on segregation. To them it made little difference whether Boutwell or Connor was mayor. It was unlikely that either candidate would represent the interests of local African Americans.

Shuttlesworth had been trying for months to convince King to bring the SCLC to Birmingham for demonstrations. In September 1962, SCLC had held a convention in Birmingham, which had worried local white leaders like Smyer who feared that the SCLC might lead protests. Local businessmen formed a group they called the Senior Citizens Committee to discuss important issues, including race. The group had invited Shuttlesworth and other black leaders to discuss the city's racial problems, hoping to avoid the kind of publicity that had been generated by the Freedom Rides. Shuttlesworth was skeptical of the efforts of the white business leaders, and he pointed out that they had not expressed any concern when his house and church had been bombed. When Shuttlesworth threatened to lead demonstrations during the convention, some members of the Senior Citizens Committee promised to continue to hold meetings to address his concerns. Although the SCLC would still hold their convention in Birmingham, Shuttlesworth agreed that there would not be any protests.

During the convention, Shuttlesworth continued to try to convince King to return to Birmingham for a large civil rights campaign. King, however, put off making a final decision. By the fall of 1962, King and the SCLC were struggling to remain relevant to the civil rights movement.

The increasing involvement of college students and other young activists after the Greensboro sit-ins and the Freedom Rides had pushed King out of the spotlight. A year earlier, the SCLC had failed in an attempt to desegregate Albany, Georgia, and some in the civil rights movement had blamed King for the lack of success.

King was only thirty-four years old when he arrived in Birmingham in the spring of 1963, but he was already in danger of becoming obsolete to the movement he had helped create. He had been thrust into the national spotlight during the Montgomery bus boycott in 1955 to 1956, when he was only twenty-six years old. Montgomery's black community chose King to become president of the Montgomery Improvement Association, the organization that led the boycott, even though King had only lived in Montgomery since

Martin Luther King Jr. (left, second seat) rides on a bus in Montgomery, Alabama, after leading a successful bus boycott for desegregation. *(Library of Congress)*

1953. But despite his inexperience, King proved to be a natural leader. His intelligence and ability to inspire people with his eloquent speeches soon made him famous.

In 1957, after the bus boycott had ended in success, King and a number of other southern black ministers created the SCLC to continue the fight for civil rights around the South. Their primary goal was to use nonviolent protests to end segregation. By using direct actions, like demonstrations and boycotts, the SCLC took a more public role than the NAACP, which largely relied on lawsuits to accomplish its goals. King and the other leaders of the SCLC hoped to get the average African American involved in civil rights activism. The SCLC struggled at first to raise money and organize effectively, but it continued to promote nonviolent protest, helping to spark boycotts and protests in several southern cities.

In 1961 in Albany, Georgia, the SCLC faced a challenge. That fall, several members of the Student Nonviolent Coordinating Committee (SNCC) began organizing protests against segregation. On November 22, the day before Thanksgiving, several students were arrested when they entered the white section of Albany's bus station. After they were jailed, other African Americans marched on city hall. Within a few weeks, more than five hundred protestors had been arrested. As the movement grew, local organizers debated whether to invite King and the SCLC to the city to help with the demonstrations. Some in Albany were afraid that they would lose control of the movement if an outside group came in and took over. Others wanted to invite King, knowing that he would bring more attention to Albany.

Protesters march outside Albany, Georgia's city hall during a movement to end segregation in the city. *(Courtesy of AP Images)*

Eventually the SCLC was invited to join the movement, and King arrived in mid-December. King was soon arrested while taking part in a march to city hall, and he said that he expected to spend Christmas in jail. Instead, King posted bail and left jail after Albany's city officials made token concessions—they would release the protestors still in jail and create a biracial group to discuss the black community's complaints. Having agreed to stop the demonstrations, King left Albany. By January, white city officials were denying that any agreement had been made, and local African Americans began protesting again. For the next eight months, protests continued sporadically, and King returned in July to face charges from his arrest in December. Little had been accomplished by August, when King and the SCLC pulled out of Albany for good.

Several problems had doomed the Albany campaign. One had been a lack of organization. There were no clear goals and little planning for how to react to mass arrests. Another problem had been the divisions within the movement. Some of the younger activists resented King's presence. With both the SCLC and SNCC working in the city, it was unclear who was in charge. Finally, Albany's police chief, Laurie Pritchett, had handled the protests without violence. He also sent many of the arrested protestors to jails outside the city, so the black community was never able to fill the jails.

Fred Shuttlesworth knew that King and the SCLC needed a victory to regain their status as effective civil rights leaders, and he invited them to Birmingham for a chance to do just that. At the same time, King wanted to avoid another disaster. With the most prominent civil rights organization struggling, the fate of the movement depended largely on achieving success in one of the South's most racist cities.

five

Struggling Toward Civil Rights

On April 3, 1963, the day after Birmingham chose Albert Boutwell over Bull Connor in the runoff election for mayor, local police arrested twenty African Americans for sitting at "whites only" lunch counters.

The sit-ins marked the beginning of one of the most important campaigns of the civil rights movements, Project "C" for "confrontation." The demonstrations, planned by the Alabama Christian Movement for Civil Rights (ACMHR) and the Southern Christian Leadership Conference (SCLC), had originally been scheduled to begin in March, but leaders had postponed them until after the runoff election for mayor. Wyatt Walker, the SCLC's executive director, had visited Birmingham in March and drawn up detailed plans for the protests. The SCLC planned to focus their efforts on local businesses rather than on the city government, hoping that they could pressure business owners into negotiations that would lead to desegregation and the hiring of more black employees at downtown stores.

The day before the sit-ins began, Walker, Shuttlesworth, and another local minister, the Reverend Nelson H. Smith Jr., wrote and circulated a document they titled the "Birmingham Manifesto." It set out the complaints of the black community and the goals of the upcoming civil rights campaign. "The patience of an oppressed people cannot endure forever," it began, before listing previous efforts to obtain basic social and economic rights. It also mentioned the violence of the Freedom Ride riots and the frequent bombings of churches and homes. Finally, it declared that "This is Birmingham's moment of truth."

Birmingham's black community was not completely united behind Project "C." Many of the city's wealthier African

Dorothy Bell, a black college student, waits at a Birmingham lunch counter for service. She was later arrested for her sit-in attempt. (*Courtesy of AP Images*)

Americans, such as A. G. Gaston, opposed the arrival of the SCLC, saying that they did not need outsiders to resolve their problems. Most of the city's ministers opposed the campaign as well, including J. L. Ware, the powerful leader of the Baptist Ministers' Conference.

The protests began in the morning on Wednesday, April 3, when seven African Americans asked to be served at Britling Cafeteria. Protestors did the same at four other lunch counters. The employees at the other lunch counters simply shut down service when the protestors sat down, but twenty were arrested at Britling Cafeteria by the end of the day.

That afternoon, King arrived in Birmingham with Ralph Abernathy. King did not yet realize how divided the black community was and expected more widespread support of the campaign. He immediately headed to a meeting of the Baptist Ministers' Conference, but he was unable to convince many of the ministers to take part in the campaign. If the movement was going to succeed, it would have to do so without the support of much of the black community's traditional leadership.

Hundreds of African Americans who did support Project "C" gathered that night in St. James Baptist Church to celebrate the beginning of the Birmingham movement. After prayers and songs, Shuttlesworth, King, and Abernathy all addressed the large crowd and promised to keep the movement going until they had won. Similar meetings would take place every night of the campaign. At the end of the night, Abernathy asked the crowd to volunteer to march and to go to jail, but only seventy-five more volunteered.

The protests the next day were smaller than hoped. Four people were arrested at a lunch counter, but other volunteers sitting at another lunch counter were simply refused service. The manager did not call police, and eventually the protestors left. Reports in the national media depicted the day's efforts as a failure.

Also on Thursday, the ACMHR and SCLC publicly issued their goals for the campaign. These included desegregation of all the stores in the downtown, including the lunch counters; more equal hiring practices, so that African Americans could be hired for white-collar jobs; the dropping of charges against protestors who had already been arrested; fairer hiring of African Americans for city jobs; and the reopening of the parks that Bull Connor had closed.

By Saturday, April 6, only thirty-five arrests had been made. The campaign was far from the all-out assault on

Shuttlesworth (front right) kneels down with other protesters during a march to Birmingham's city hall. The police eventually stopped this march and arrested forty-two of the participants. *(Library of Congress)*

segregation promised by King and Shuttlesworth. Hoping to create more excitement, and more arrests, the leaders decided to try a march instead of relying on sit-ins. Shuttlesworth led a group of protestors toward city hall. About three blocks from their destination, the police stopped the march and arrested forty-two of the participants. At the nightly meeting, King said that there was much more to come, and that he was ready to go to jail.

Violence erupted for the first time during a march the next day. After a church service, the Reverend A. D. King, Martin Luther King's brother and a minister at a local church, led a large group of African Americans on another attempt to walk to city hall. As police began arresting the marchers, a police dog attacked a young black man, Leroy Allen, who

Birmingham policemen often used police dogs to break up civil rights marches. *(Courtesy of AP Images/Bill Hudson)*

was watching the march. Police broke up the confrontation quickly, but not until the dog had bitten the spectator and knocked him to the ground. Allen was arrested along with more than twenty marchers. As they made their arrests, the police also broke up the crowd with their night sticks.

Finally, this attack attracted considerable attention from the national media. Noticing the increased coverage, Wyatt Walker, who had helped plan the protests, grew excited and hoped to provoke more confrontations.

The movement had succeeded in getting noticed, but there was still a lack of volunteers. King spent the next two days trying to get more of the black community involved. He appealed again to the city's black ministers and tried to convince them to become active in the campaign. On Tuesday, April 9, King addressed more than one hundred local black businessmen to recruit them into the movement. The businessmen did not promise to become more active, but they did announce that they would at least not oppose King and the SCLC. Their statement allowed the movement's leaders to claim that the black community was united behind them, even if the support was not very enthusiastic.

While King was trying to raise support for the demonstrations, the city's white leaders were looking for a way to end them. With the help of the state government, Birmingham's officials were able to get the maximum bail for arrested protestors raised from three hundred dollars to twenty-five hundred dollars, making it much more difficult to get protestors out of jail if they were arrested. The SCLC was already running out of bail money, and the increase could potentially bankrupt the movement. The city and state leaders also discussed how to handle the protestors. Bull Connor and Alabama governor

George Wallace, who had recently been elected based on his promise to enforce segregation, wanted to let the police use brutal tactics to end the demonstrations, but Birmingham's white business leaders argued that it was more effective to use a gentler approach.

On Wednesday, city officials again maneuvered to stop the demonstrations. A state judge agreed to issue a temporary injunction that made it illegal to take part in future protests. Before the injunction, the activists could claim that they had the law on their side and were just trying to exercise their rights. That was no longer the case. King responded by saying that he and the other civil rights leaders would not respect the injunction: "We can not in all good conscience obey an injunction which is an unjust, undemocratic and unconstitutional misuse of the legal process." And, said King, he was ready to march and go to jail.

Small sit-ins and protests continued that week, but there were still too few volunteers to hold massive demonstrations. The campaign's leaders knew that they were low on funds and had to decide how to continue. King had said that he would lead a march on Friday, April 12, but he considered leaving the city to go north to raise money. All of the available options had significant drawbacks. After discussing the dire situation with the movement's other leaders, King decided to go through with the march scheduled for Friday. He would go to jail and hope that his arrest might spark more interest.

six

Keeping the Campaign Alive

On Friday afternoon, King, Abernathy, and about fifty other marchers were arrested as they made their way toward city hall. Hundreds of other African Americans crowded along the streets to witness the confrontation. King and Abernathy were shoved roughly into a police wagon and taken to jail, where they were held in solitary confinement away from the other prisoners.

Police kept King from having much contact with the outside world while he was imprisoned, but he did get some good news. His lawyer, Clarence Jones told him that the popular singer Harry Belafonte had raised $50,000 for bail money. King could stop worrying that perhaps he should have raised money instead of going to jail. He heard more good news when he was finally allowed to talk to his wife, Coretta Scott King. Coretta told him that President Kennedy had called her with his support. King and the other leaders

Police officers arrest King (left) and Abernathy during their march toward city hall. *(Courtesy of AP Images/Horace Cort)*

of the movement took this as a sign that the federal government might be ready to become involved on their behalf.

King used the time in jail to write the long letter that would eventually become famous. He explained the reasons that he had come to Birmingham, writing that "injustice anywhere is a threat to justice everywhere." He agreed that it was unfortunate that the demonstrations had to take place, but said that the black community had "no other alternative." To justify the demonstrations, King pointed out that the white city leaders had always ignored the complaints of Birmingham's African Americans. In a passage that reflects King's use of dramatic language and philosophical references, he explained the reason that negotiation alone was not enough:

> You may well ask: 'Why direct action? Why sit-ins, marches,

An officer prepares to put King in a police wagon after King's arrest during a march toward city hall. *(Library of Congress)*

and so forth? Isn't negotiation a better path?' You are quite right in calling for negotiation. Indeed this is the very purpose of direct action. Nonviolent direct action seeks to create such a crisis and foster such a tension that a community which has constantly refused to negotiate is forced to confront the issue. . . . My citing the creation of tension as part of the work of the nonviolent resister may sound rather shocking. But I must confess that I am not afraid of the word "tension." I have earnestly opposed violent tension, but there is a type of constructive, nonviolent tension which is necessary for growth. Just as Socrates felt that it was necessary to create a tension in the mind so that individuals could rise from the bondage of myths and half-truths to the unfettered realm of creative analysis and objective appraisal, we must see the need for nonviolent gadflies to create the kind of tension in society that will help men rise from the dark depths of prejudice and racism to the majestic heights of understanding and brotherhood.

Then King warned his readers that it was better to negotiate with civil rights leaders than to risk pushing African

Americans into violence. "Oppressed people cannot remain oppressed forever," wrote King. "The yearning for freedom eventually manifests itself, and that is what has happened to the American Negro." So, said King, African Americans should be allowed to protest so that their frustration did not take a more violent turn:

> The Negro has many pent-up resentments and latent frustrations, and he must release them. So let him march; let him make prayer pilgrimages to city hall; let him go on freedom rides—and try to understand why he must do so. If his repressed emotions are not released in nonviolent ways, they will seek expression through violence.

While King sat behind bars composing his letter, protests continued. Six young African American men were arrested

Harry Belafonte, seen here speaking at a civil rights rally, raised $50,000 for bail money to support the marches in Birmingham. *(Library of Congress)*

on Saturday, April 13, after picketing a store and then asking for service at its lunch counter. On Sunday, violence broke out after more peaceful marchers were arrested. After leaving church, a group of activists marched toward the jail. Bull Connor ordered the marchers arrested, which angered a large group of African American bystanders, who began throwing rocks at the police. One young African American was caught by several policemen, beaten to the ground, and held down. About thirty of the marchers were arrested, as well as a few of the bystanders.

On Monday, the new city government, led by Mayor Albert Boutwell, was sworn into office. But the city commissioners—Bull Connor, Art Hanes, and J. T. Waggoner—refused to leave office. Their appeal of the change in city government had not yet been decided by the courts, and they still maintained that they should be able to serve out their terms. So, as of April 15, Birmingham had two city governments. The two sides worked out a compromise—both governments would hold office until the legal challenge was decided. Boutwell did not directly mention the demonstrations in his speech at the swearing-in ceremony, but he did make it clear that the new government would not be much more sympathetic to the civil rights protests than the old government. "Whatever our shortcomings may be, they are our own local problems and we shall resolve them by local effort and local unity," he said. "We shall not submit to the intimidations of pressure."

With two city governments now looking on, demonstrations continued, but participation remained lower than the movement's leaders had hoped. King's arrest had sparked more coverage from the national media, but it had not led to the massive protests that the SCLC and ACMHR had hoped for. On Wednesday, about fifteen African Americans were arrested for being part of a march to the county courthouse to register to vote. They had gathered first at a local church to go over the necessary steps for registration and planned to go as a group to the courthouse. But the police chief, Jamie Moore, warned them that if they marched as a group, they would be arrested. When they marched despite the warning, Moore fulfilled his promise and had them taken to jail.

Leaders of the campaign hoped that the arrests would lead to federal intervention. Up to this point, President Kennedy's administration had said that it had no justification for becoming directly involved because it was a local, not a federal, matter. But, preventing people from registering to vote could potentially give Kennedy a reason to intervene. And the civil rights leaders knew that if they were going to be successful, ultimately they would need the assistance of the federal government.

On Saturday, after eight days in jail, King and Abernathy posted bail. The campaign was still struggling, and they hoped that they would be able to do more for it once they were no longer behind bars. Both were optimistic when they spoke to the press after their release. They declared that the black community was supportive of the campaign, and that the boycott of downtown stores had been very effective. They also announced that they were willing to negotiate, but that the campaign would not end until they had achieved their goals.

Although King did not yet know it, steps taken by another civil rights leader during the week that King spent in jail would eventually make victory possible. James Bevel, a minister and experienced civil rights activist, had arrived in town on the day of King's arrest and had preached at the mass meeting that night. While King was in jail, Bevel began holding workshops with students after school, teaching them about the civil rights movement and about how to protest. The meetings of local students quickly became popular and many of the students showed great enthusiasm for the movement.

James Bevel *(Library of Congress)*

When King, Shuttlesworth, and the other movement leaders began preparing for more protests, Bevel urged them to allow high school students, and even elementary school students, to take part in the demonstrations. The movement leaders finally agreed to let Bevel have his way. It would be up to the city's children to save the campaign.

seven
Saved by the Students

It was not an easy decision to allow young students to face Bull Connor's police dogs and fire hoses. On Monday, April 29, King met with other leaders of the SCLC and ACMHR to discuss what to do next. It was then that Bevel suggested allowing the students he had been meeting with to join the demonstrations. The workshops had sparked excitement among them, and they were numerous; perhaps the movement could finally fulfill its promise to fill the jails. King and several others were hesitant to enlist the help of children. Not only would it put the students in harm's way, it would also risk angering their parents.

After a long discussion, it was decided that the students would be allowed to march. Now the only question was when. On Tuesday, Shuttlesworth made a request for a permit to conduct a protest on Thursday, but both city governments turned him down. Mayor Boutwell claimed that allowing a

Policemen direct a group of black children to jail after their arrest for marching against racial discrimination. *(Courtesy of AP Images/Bill Hudson)*

protest might lead to public disorder. With the permit request denied, any student who took part in a demonstration would be breaking the law.

That week, activists distributed leaflets at the city's black high schools that told the students to meet on Thursday at a local church to prepare for a demonstration, even if their parents, teachers, or principals told them not to go. They were also told to bring their toothbrushes—they would need them in jail. Because the campaign's leaders were worried that parents might oppose allowing the students to march, they did not mention the upcoming demonstration at the nightly meetings.

When Thursday finally arrived, local students skipped school to meet at the Sixteenth Street Baptist Church. Some parents arrived, angry at King for allowing their children to march. Although King was uneasy about the decision, the students showed little hesitation as they sang and clapped in the church.

At noon, the march began. The city's white leaders had known since they denied the permit request that a large demonstration would be taking place, and they were prepared. Police were waiting as the young activists stepped out of the church and began marching toward city hall and downtown stores. The students left the church in groups of ten to fifty. They were soon met by police, who herded them into police wagons. When the police ran out of wagons, they began using school buses to take the students to jail. Bystanders noticed that most of the students seemed happy—they laughed and sang on their way into police vehicles. Some ran when they spotted police, but many others simply surrendered without any opposition.

Birmingham police arrested so many young marchers that they were forced to use school buses to transport prisoners to jail. *(Courtesy of AP Images)*

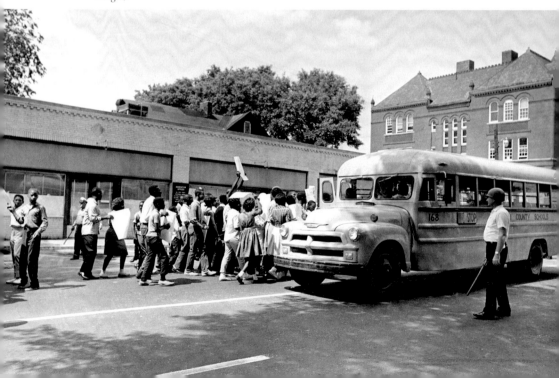

Bull Connor ordered fire engines to wait at several street corners, and the fire hoses were brought out but not turned on. The police also refrained from using police dogs, hoping to avoid any outcry over the treatment of the children. Many of the marchers were high school students, but there were some who were much younger. One girl even told a reporter as she was led onto a police wagon that she was only six years old. None of the protestors made it all the way to city hall, but three groups did reach the downtown shopping area before being arrested. King and other leaders of the movement waited and monitored the protests from the Gaston Hotel, not far from the Sixteenth Street Baptist Church.

By four o'clock the streets were empty. Inside the jails, cells that normally held eight prisoners now held more than seventy-five. Despite the tension, there had been no violence. At night, 2,000 people gathered at the Sixth Avenue Baptist Church to celebrate the success of the day's protest. King estimated that 958 children had marched and about six hundred had been arrested and now sat in jail. "I have been inspired and moved today," said King. "I have never seen anything like it." The courage of the students had revitalized the movement and inspired the adults. The white community was not so enthusiastic, arguing that King was exploiting the children for the purposes of the campaign.

On Friday, Connor was determined to stop the demonstrations. That morning, he had fire trucks and policemen line key streets to try to stop the marches before they could get going. More than one thousand students showed up at Sixteenth Street Baptist Church to take part. There were also hundreds of spectators watching from a nearby park.

At about one in the afternoon, the first of the students began marching out of the church. With the jail already full, Connor's goal was to stop the demonstrations, not to arrest hundreds more. But in the first hour, about seventy students were arrested, and more students kept emerging from the church. To stop the seemingly endless flow of protestors, Connor ordered police to begin spraying the students with high-powered fire hoses.

A police officer ordered one group of about sixty marchers to disperse or else they would be hit with the hoses. The students kept marching, and the police turned on the water. At first they used only half pressure, hoping to discourage the students. When they kept going, the water pressure was turned higher, knocking down several of the students.

As the media spread pictures of water hoses being used against young protesters, the actions of Birmingham authorities began to garner national condemnation. *(Courtesy of AP Images/Bill Hudson)*

The hoses were so intense that one student had his shirt ripped off by the water. When A. G. Gaston looked out the window of his office, he saw the police turning the hoses on one young protestor. "They've turned the fire hoses on a little black girl," he exclaimed. "And they're rolling that girl right down the middle of the street." The songs quickly turned to screams.

Angered by the use of the hoses, some African American onlookers began throwing rocks and bottles at the police. The police responded by using dogs to try to subdue the crowds, and three students wound up in the hospital with injuries caused by dog bites. Meanwhile, new waves of marchers continued to come out of the church. Many avoided the area of confrontation only to be picked up by school buses and arrested.

By three o'clock in the afternoon, hundreds of students still remained ready to march, but the streets were growing more dangerous. A police inspector entered the church and warned the civil rights leaders that the crowd of bystanders had become restless. King agreed to end the demonstrations for the day, hoping to avoid a riot. About 250 students had been arrested by the time the marches were halted.

Mayor Boutwell condemned the protests, saying that students should not be involved in dangerous activities. But King and Shuttlesworth announced that the protests would continue. "If the white power structure of this city will meet some of our minimum demands, then we will consider calling off the demonstrations," said King, "but we want promises, plus action."

Although the marches had been called off earlier than originally planned, they were a great success for the campaign. Media coverage spread pictures of policemen using water hoses on young children, bringing condemnation from around the country and the world. In Washington, President John F. Kennedy and Attorney General Robert F. Kennedy realized that the negative publicity would seriously damage the image of the United States if the violence was not stopped. Robert Kennedy issued a statement in which he tried to show an understanding of both sides without angering either. He wrote that "Continued refusal to grant equal rights and opportunities to Negroes makes increasing turmoil inevitable." But he also criticized the civil rights campaign: "the timing of the present demonstrations is open to question. School children participating in street demonstrations is a dangerous business. An injured, maimed or dead child is a price that none of us can afford to pay."

To try to find a resolution, the Kennedys sent Burke Marshall, the assistant attorney general for civil rights, to Birmingham to try to negotiate a truce. Marshall called King to ask that the demonstrations be halted, but King refused. That night, hundreds of African Americans gathered again at the Sixteenth Street Baptist Church and heard King and Andrew Young warn against throwing rocks or turning to other types of violence. The civil rights leaders knew that they would have the moral high ground, and positive media coverage, as long as Connor and the police were seen as the ones causing the violence. The success of the two days of student marches was drawing the black community together and uniting them against the repressive tactics of the white city government.

Later that night, negotiations began again between the white and black community. Sidney Smyer led a group of

Burke Marshall, the assistant attorney general for civil rights, was sent to Birmingham to negotiate a truce. *(Library of Congress)*

white businessmen in an attempt to reach an agreement that would end the demonstrations. The black community was represented by some traditional leaders, such as attorney Arthur Shores and A. G. Gaston, and by some leaders of the civil rights campaign, such as Shuttlesworth and Andrew Young. The boycott was hurting white businessmen, as the protests were keeping both white and black shoppers away from downtown. The white businessmen did not represent the city government, so their power was limited, but they could at least negotiate over the desegregation of local businesses. Although nothing was resolved at first, these meetings would continue over the next few days as the two sides tried to find common ground.

King and Walker came up with a new strategy for Saturday's protests. Students were sent in small groups of two or three from two different churches. After getting close to city hall or downtown stores, the marchers would meet up again. Hundreds of demonstrators made it into the streets using these new tactics. They had found a way around Connor's attempt to keep them bottled up near the church.

Connor responded by sending police to the churches to prevent any more demonstrators from leaving. With the non-violent protestors trapped inside the churches, the large crowd gathered in a nearby park again began throwing rocks at the police. The police began using dogs and fire hoses to try to disperse the crowd, triggering another barrage of rocks and bottles. James Bevel used a bullhorn to ask the crowd to leave. As the onlookers gradually began to drift off, Bevel announced that demonstrations would end for the day. Soon after, campaign leaders announced a one-day moratorium on demonstrations. The day's arrests brought the total for the three days of student protests to more than 1,100.

Although there were no official demonstrations on Sunday, May 5, a group of African American churchgoers attempted to march to the jail for a prayer meeting after a church service. As they drew closer, however, fire trucks and policemen pulled up and blocked their path. The firemen prepared to turn on their hoses, but the well-dressed crowd refused to turn around. One of the march's leaders, the Reverend Charles Billups, called out to the firemen "Turn on your water! Turn loose your dogs! We will stand here 'til we die!"

A fireman manning the hose froze, unable or unwilling to spray the crowd, despite Bull Connor's order to turn on the hose. Wyatt Walker whispered to two police captains that they could defuse the confrontation by allowing the marchers to pray in the park across the street. The police agreed, and the showdown ended. To those in the march, it was a victory: they had stared down the fire hoses and won.

Martin Luther King left Birmingham for the weekend to return to his church in Atlanta and lead the church service. He spoke to his congregation about the protests and declared that he was confident that the campaign would succeed. He also discussed the importance of success in Birmingham for the entire civil rights movement: "If we can crack Birmingham, I am convinced we can crack the South. Birmingham is a symbol of segregation for the entire South." Speaking in Jackson, Mississippi, Alabama's governor, George Wallace, had a very different take on the protests. He said that most residents of Birmingham, both black and white, opposed the protests and wanted them to stop. He also blamed the demonstrations on "left wing" outsiders.

With the protests gathering steam, and the boycott and negative press hurting Birmingham's businesses, local white businessmen hoped to reach a resolution that would end the demonstrations. They set up a meeting with their African American counterparts for Sunday night. These meetings were held late at night and kept as quiet as possible because the white businessmen knew that many white residents would oppose any effort to negotiate with the protestors, and they hoped to avoid a backlash. A. G. Gaston restated the movement's goals: the desegregation of stores and lunch counters, better employment opportunities for African Americans, the dropping of charges against those already arrested, and the creation of a biracial committee to discuss other problems.

But the meeting broke down when the white businessmen refused to discuss the second two points. Burke Marshall represented the administration in this meeting, and he urged the two sides to continue talking.

The next morning, Marshall met with King to try to convince him to call off the demonstrations scheduled for that afternoon. Marshall argued that further protests would only make it more difficult to reach an agreement. He asked King to wait until the courts had ruled on the challenge to the new city government before resuming protests, so that the new city government could take part in negotiations. King, however, pointed out that the businessmen had not yet made any serious concessions; he would not stop the demonstrations.

eight
An Uneasy Truce

If Sidney Smyer and other white businessmen thought that things could not get worse, Monday's demonstrations would change their minds. Schools were empty as more than one thousand black students skipped class to march for civil rights. The campaign passed around flyers to the students that told them that they were responsible for the future of African Americans: "Join the thousand in jail who are making their witness for freedom. . . . It's up to you to free our teachers, our parents, yourself and our country."

Around noon, popular African American comedian Dick Gregory, who had come to town to participate in the protests, led the first group of nineteen students out of the Sixteenth Street Baptist Church. The police were waiting outside, and a police captain warned the protestors that they would be arrested if they continued. When the marchers kept moving, police began ushering the singing students onto buses to take them to jail.

Young black students effectively paralyzed the downtown area of Birmingham with protests, sit-ins, and picket lines. *(Library of Congress)*

This time, more than half of the protestors were adults—some of them even went to jail with their children. After two hours and hundreds of arrests, tempers began to flare. Some bystanders began throwing rocks and bottles at police. Just before three o'clock, King called off the protests. He did not want to risk having the protest turn into a riot.

The day had already been a successful one, with more than one thousand arrests. The headline in the *New York Times* the next day reflected the campaign's success: "Birmingham Jails 1,000 More Negroes." Having run out of space in the jail, police began moving those arrested to the state fairgrounds, holding them in large outdoor pens. The day's arrests moved

Police were forced to move the prisoners to the state fairgrounds as the Birmingham jails became too crowded to hold them. *(Courtesy of AP Images/Bill Hudson)*

the total for the campaign close to 2,500, and the movement's leaders promised that the demonstrations would continue.

So many people attended the mass meeting that night that they filled four churches. King made his way to all four to speak to the overflowing crowds. His speeches celebrated the recent successes and encouraged those listening to continue to take part in the protests. He also reassured parents that their children would be okay.

Later that night, Burke Marshall and King discussed the possibility of ending the demonstrations temporarily to allow more time for negotiations, and Smyer's group of white businessmen told King that they would desegregate department stores and lunch counters in return for an end to the protests. But the movement's leaders turned down the offer, saying it was not enough to justify ending the demonstrations.

Both civil rights leaders and city officials knew Tuesday's protests would be crucial. King and Shuttlesworth hoped to avoid having marchers arrested so quickly this time, so they had demonstrators meet in small groups across the city to picket stores. The plan then called for the small groups to meet downtown to form a large protest.

That morning, students left from locations all over the city and headed toward downtown. The plan worked, and Connor and other city officials were caught by surprise. Back at the Sixteenth Street Baptist Church, Wyatt Walker waited until many of the police outside the church had been drawn away by calls for more police to arrest the protestors already downtown and then began sending groups out of the church. Students leaving the church sprinted past police barriers. This time they would not surrender to arrest so easily.

Young black students were everywhere—blocking traffic, sitting at "whites only" lunch counters, picketing stores. With the police in disarray, the campaign had succeeded in paralyzing the city. In the early afternoon, many of the protestors began returning to the church as planned for another assault. The hope was that finally the campaign would be able to force the city to meet its demands.

By three that afternoon, however, the protests had begun to turn violent. Local African Americans who were not part of the campaign became excited by the success of the protestors and joined in, but they did not all have the same commitment to nonviolence. Police began using fire hoses and night sticks to subdue protestors, and Bull Connor grew increasingly angry. State police soon arrived in the city and viciously beat protestors and onlookers alike. Fred Shuttlesworth was caught by a fire hose and slammed against a brick wall. An ambulance took him to a local hospital, inspiring Connor to remark later that "I wish they'd carried him away in a hearse." There were few arrests, as police attempted to disperse the crowd rather than arrest protestors. By four o'clock, the streets finally began clearing.

The day's chaotic protests again made headlines across the country. The *New York Times* reported that so many people had been arrested over the past few days that it took more than four hours to serve all the prisoners breakfast. Cells were so crowded that prisoners had to sleep next to each other on the floor with little room to spare. Because of the lack of space, local officials even began releasing young prisoners to their parents without cash bonds.

The editor of the local paper, the *Birmingham News*, sent a telegram to President Kennedy that was then printed on the front page the next day. The telegram asked the president to intervene to end the demonstrations, saying that the protestors had shown "open defiance of uniformed police officers." The editor had little sympathy for the complaints of the black community and said that the protestors were endangering all of the city's residents. Other white leaders, however, were more skeptical about federal intervention and wanted to settle the matter locally. They knew that if the federal government did become involved, it might force the local government to give in to some of the black community's demands.

While Birmingham's streets filled with protestors and policemen, about seventy-five white business leaders gathered in the local Chamber of Commerce to discuss how to put an end to the demonstrations. Mayor Albert Boutwell also attended, showing that, unlike Connor, he was willing to negotiate if it would restore order. Some favored imposing martial law and using force as soon as possible. Others realized that it was the use of force that had brought so much negative attention to the city already and argued for negotiations. As the demonstrations grew into a riot outside, those gathered in the Chamber of Commerce finally settled on a number of concessions that they were willing to make if it would end the protests.

That night, some of the business leaders presented their offer to the African American negotiating committee. After some positive discussion, they took the proposal to King. Eventually, the two sides were able to come to an agreement. Department store dressing rooms would be immediately desegregated. Lunch counters would be desegregated within sixty days. The business leaders also agreed to hire at least some black employees at downtown stores and to set concrete goals for further hiring. Other aspects of the black community's initial demands that needed the approval of the city government would be discussed when the new city government officially took over. Finally, a biracial committee would be created to address other issues in the future. But there was still one sticking point—they could not agree whether charges should be dropped against the jailed protestors. When the meeting finally ended at three in the morning, there was hope that a final settlement would soon be reached.

On Wednesday morning, the leaders of the campaign gathered to discuss the negotiations. Shuttlesworth, however, was still in the hospital. King eventually announced that he would agree to a one-day moratorium on protests to see if a final settlement could be reached. When Shuttlesworth found out, he was furious. As soon as he left the hospital, he went to King and confronted him, angrily condemning him for giving in. But after Shuttlesworth and King talked privately, they reached an agreement and Shuttlesworth seemed at least somewhat supportive of the compromise.

On Thursday, King postponed the deadline while discussions continued. He also seemed more willing to compromise on the campaign's goals. That night, the two sides reached a final agreement. King, Abernathy, and Shuttlesworth held a press conference to announce the truce. The final agreement called for the desegregation of lunch counters, restrooms, dressing rooms, and water fountains within ninety days; fair hiring of African Americans, including the hiring

King (left), Shuttlesworth (center), and Abernathy hold a news conference to announce the desegregation demands accepted by city leaders. *(Courtesy of AP Images)*

of clerks and salesmen within sixty days and further discussion of more progress in hiring; the release on bail of all the protestors still in jail; and the creation of a biracial committee within two weeks. After he read the text of the agreement, Shuttlesworth collapsed. The effort and stress of the monthlong campaign had exhausted him, and he was taken back to the hospital.

King then made his own statement celebrating the success of the civil rights campaign. King praised Shuttlesworth for his years of activism, and he also thanked the white businessmen who had been willing to negotiate. He said that the agreement would allow everyone to "look forward now to continued progress toward the establishment of a city in which equal job opportunities, equal access to public facilities, and equal rights and responsibilities for all of its people will be the order of every day." There was still a lot of work to be done, warned King, but the compromise was a "great victory."

The compromise ended demonstrations for the moment, but it appeared to be a tenuous agreement. Sidney Smyer was the only one of the white businessmen willing to sign his name to the agreement. The others were too worried about white residents who might oppose the deal. And although he had been part of some of the discussions, Albert Boutwell said that he had nothing to do with them. "I'm unwilling to make decisions virtually at gunpoint or as the result of agitation," he said. Birmingham's other mayor, Art Hanes, was even more outspoken against the agreement. Hanes declared that if the white businessmen would stop negotiating, "we would run King and that bunch of race agitators out of town."

nine
Backlash

Hanes was not the only one upset by the agreement. On the night of Saturday, May 11, just a day after the settlement was announced, 2,500 members of the Ku Klux Klan listened to Robert Shelton, the leader of Georgia's Klan, condemn the agreement. Shelton declared that the Klan should fight the truce.

Later that night, shortly before eleven o'clock, the Klan struck. Two bombs ripped apart the house of A. D. King. The Klan had apparently wanted to kill Martin Luther King and thought he might be at his brother's house. But Martin had returned to Atlanta to preach at his church the next day, and A. D. King's family escaped without serious injury. A large crowd began gathering outside the house, angry about the attack. When police arrived, some in the crowd began throwing rocks and slashing the tires of police cars.

Not long after the bombing at A. D. King's house, another bomb went off at the Gaston Motel, where Martin Luther

Robert Shelton, the leader of Georgia's Ku Klux Klan, declared that the Klan should fight desegregation in Birmingham. *(Library of Congress)*

King had been staying. An even larger crowd gathered after this explosion. The arrival of police again touched off their anger, and a riot quickly broke out. At least one policeman was stabbed, and several others were hit by objects thrown from the crowd. A car was set on fire outside the Sixteenth Street Baptist Church. White-owned stores were also torched and looted.

A. D. King arrived and tried to disperse the rioters, using a megaphone to plead with people to leave:

Damage caused by the Gaston Hotel bombing *(Library of Congress)*

> Our home was just bombed. . . . Now if we who were in jeopardy of being killed, if we have gone away not angry, not throwing bricks, if we could do that and we were in danger, why must you rise up to hurt our cause? You are hurting us! You are not helping! Now won't you please clear this park.

Wyatt Walker had also tried to help calm the crowd, but he was beaten by state police, and his wrist was fractured. By the end of the night several buildings had been destroyed, as well as a number of cars. Dozens of African Americans were injured and taken to the hospital. The Gaston Hotel had suffered major damage. A large hole in the wall had opened the reception area to the outside.

Wyatt Walker stands on a car with a megaphone in an attempt to calm the crowd gathered to protest the bombing attacks on the Gaston Motel and A. D. King's house. *(Courtesy of AP Images)*

On Sunday, Martin Luther King cut short his trip to Atlanta and flew back to Birmingham. He said that "I do not feel that the events of last night nullified the agreement at all." Mayor Boutwell issued a stating saying that "this city will not tolerate violence."

In Washington, John and Robert Kennedy began worrying that the bombing and riots would put an end to the halt on demonstrations. That Wednesday, at an afternoon press conference, President Kennedy said the government "would use all available means to protect human rights and uphold the law of the land." He also urged "the local leaders of Birmingham, both white and Negro, to continue their constructive and cooperative efforts."

Alabama governor George Wallace (right) criticized the white business leaders who had negotiated with the civil rights activists. Wallace stands beside Birmingham mayor Albert Boutwell. *(Library of Congress)*

George Wallace also issued a statement condemning the bombings. Most of his statement, however, was spent blaming King and the SCLC for provoking violence. Wallace also criticized the white business leaders who had negotiated with the civil rights leaders. He claimed that they had made maintaining law and order even more difficult by offering concessions to protestors who had broken the law. Wallace responded to Kennedy's decision to send soldiers into Alabama by saying that the state did not need the federal government's help to maintain the peace, and he questioned whether it was legal for the president to send the troops. The next day, Kennedy replied to Wallace that he hoped he would not have to order the military into Birmingham, but that it would depend on whether the state and local government could prevent further bombings and violence.

Also on Monday, King visited pool halls and bars to try to convince local African Americans not to resort to violence, even when provoked. At a meeting that night at Sixth Avenue Baptist Church, boxer Floyd Patterson, and Jackie Robinson, the first African American to play Major League Baseball, spoke to the crowd and thanked them for what they had done for the civil rights movement. When King spoke, he reaffirmed his commitment to the agreement and said that "I'm sorry, but I will never teach any of you to hate white people."

White business leaders who had taken part in the negotiations with the SCLC and ACMHR also decided that they needed to save the agreement. On Wednesday, May 15, the group finally made all the names of the members public, and issued a statement explaining why the members had decided to negotiate. They said they believed that desegregation was inevitable, and that it would be better to desegregate peacefully and avoid violence. But the statement also said that some members of the committee did not agree with the final settlement that had ended the demonstrations. The question now was whether that meant that they would not honor the agreement. If they did not, the civil rights campaign would not yet be able to claim victory.

When the leaders of the local civil rights movement saw the statement, they responded by saying that they needed to clarify exactly what the business leaders meant. King said that he understood that, under the agreement, the seven stores that had been part of the negotiations would all hire at least one African American in a sales position. But Sidney

Smyer claimed that only one African American had to be promoted to a sales position in any one of the stores. Despite the disagreement, King reaffirmed that he was committed to maintaining the truce. When the weekend passed without violence, it seemed that perhaps the long ordeal was winding down.

On Monday, May 20, however, another problem arose. The city's board of education announced that more than one thousand African American students would be expelled from school for taking part in the demonstrations, even though there were less than two weeks left in the school year. Civil rights leaders declared that they would go to court to try to get the students reinstated. The board of education's decision was quickly overturned by a federal judge and the students were able to return to classes.

Another important legal ruling was announced the same week. The Alabama Supreme Court denied the challenge by the old city government, including Art Hanes and Bull Connor. Mayor Boutwell and the city council could now officially take office. The ruling ended Connor's long career at the center of Birmingham politics. Although Boutwell was also committed to segregation, it was still an important change. Connor represented the hard-line segregationists who would use any means, including violence, to maintain old Jim Crow laws. Connor's loss symbolized the changing times—segregation could not last forever.

Progress would be slow in coming, but the civil rights campaign in Birmingham in 1963 put the city on the path to integration. The movement was also successful in inspiring other campaigns across the South. Demonstrations erupted in hundreds of cities. Within a month of the Birmingham agreement, close to 15,000 protestors had been arrested for taking part in civil rights demonstrations elsewhere. The campaign also returned King and the SCLC to prominence. In the weeks after the agreement, King toured the North and raised unprecedented amounts of money for the civil rights movement. His "Letter from Birmingham Jail" was reprinted in a number of newspapers and magazines, bringing his thoughts on nonviolent protest to the nation. At a large rally in California, the SCLC raised $75,000. Another rally in Chicago raised $40,000. The success in Birmingham also provided the SCLC with a model for future demonstrations in other cities. They had cracked one of the toughest cities in the South.

In late August, the civil rights movement launched one of the most impressive demonstrations in American history. More than 200,000 people, both black and white, gathered in Washington, D.C. to rally for equal rights. Popular musicians such as Joan Baez and Peter, Paul, and Mary played for the crowd, and a number of civil rights leaders gave speeches celebrating what had been accomplished and discussing how much was still left to do. Fred Shuttlesworth and Martin Luther King both spoke.

As he often did, King referred to both the Bible and American history to argue that African Americans deserved to have the same rights as white Americans. He said that it had been one hundred years since Abraham Lincoln had issued the Emancipation Proclamation and still African Americans were not free.

"Now," he said, "is the time to make justice a reality for all of God's children. . . . There will be neither rest nor tranquility in America until the Negro is granted his citizenship rights. The whirlwinds of revolt will continue to shake the foundations of our nation until the bright day of justice emerges."

King continued with what has become one of the most famous passages in American history. "I have a dream," he declared: that one day this nation will rise up and live out the true meaning of its creed: 'We hold these truths to be self-evident: that all men are created equal.'

Finally, King ended by proclaiming that when equality was finally achieved and all Americans were given their rights, then they would be able to say "Free at last! Free at last! Thank God Almighty, we are free at last!"

King gives his now-famous "I Have A Dream" speech during a civil rights demonstration in Washington, D.C. *(Courtesy of the Department of Defense)*

ten
The Legacy of Birmingham

Back in Birmingham, the next few weeks would show that King's dream was still a long way from becoming reality. For much of the summer the city was fairly calm, at least compared to the tension of April and March. But as a new school year drew near, the possibility of school integration reignited violence.

In June and July, it looked as though race relations were steadily improving. Three of the golf courses that had been closed by Bull Connor more than a year earlier reopened in late June, and both blacks and whites were able to use them. The local library was also desegregated, and in July sit-ins succeeded in integrating a number of restaurants and lunch counters.

When it came to the public schools, however, many white residents still felt strongly that segregation should be maintained. In July, a federal court ordered Birmingham to submit a plan to desegregate its schools. At least some of the public schools would have to be integrated when the school year began in September. The school board responded by submitting a plan for limited integration, and the plan was approved by the courts. But for some white Birmingham residents, even partial desegregation was too much, and they began trying to convince local officials to close the schools rather than integrate them. Some in the black community were upset as well because they felt that all the schools should be integrated as soon as possible and that the city's plan was too limited.

As the start of the school year approached, the city grew tense with apprehension. On August 21, the home of Arthur Shores, a lawyer arguing for integration, was bombed. The attack on his home showed how strongly some white residents opposed school integration. No one knew exactly what would happen when the first black students attempted to enter schools that had long been all-white. Some thought that Governor Wallace might intervene and close the schools; others feared that integration would result in more violence.

School was scheduled to begin on Wednesday, September 4. Two high schools and one elementary school that had been all-white were to admit a few black students each. On September 2, Governor Wallace temporarily closed schools in two other cities that had been scheduled to integrate. Wallace sent more than one hundred state policemen to a school in Tuskegee, Alabama, to ensure that the school could not be opened. It was thought that he might try to do something similar in Birmingham.

When Wednesday arrived, two black children successfully registered at an all-white elementary school. White demonstrators near the schools carried Confederate flags

Birmingham students protest school integration after two black students were admitted to their high school. *(Courtesy of AP Images)*

and yelled at police, but school officials allowed the students to register. They would start classes the next day, as would several high school students at another school. But that night, another bomb was set off, again at the home of Arthur Shores, which was still damaged from the bombing a few weeks earlier. When police arrived, a number of local black residents confronted them, and some began throwing rocks and bottles. The police responded by using force to push the residents back into their homes. After two hours, the conflict was finally over, but a twenty-year-old African American man had been shot and killed by police, and more than a dozen other local residents were injured.

The next day, before three Birmingham schools could become the first integrated public schools in the state, the board of education canceled classes at Wallace's request. Lawyers for the black students immediately sued to over-turn the decision, but at least for this day there would be no school integration. Wallace had built his political career on his opposition to desegregation, and once again he had fulfilled his promise to prevent integration when-ever possible.

The battle over the schools continued into the next week. On Tuesday, September 11, after a court ordered the schools to reopen, Birmingham's schools were finally integrated. Of course, only a few black students attended the previously all-white schools, but it still represented a major change. Wallace had done everything he could to prevent the black students from integrating the schools. He even ordered the Alabama National Guard into the city to prevent desegregation. But President Kennedy responded by taking control of the sol-diers and allowing the schools to open.

As two African American girls entered one of the local high schools on Tuesday morning, white students began leaving the school in protest of the integration. Some white students collected near the entrance to the school and began yelling at the black students. "Go home!" they shouted. And "Two, four, six, eight, we don't want to integrate." Some of the white parents also jeered the black students and called for the white students still inside the school to leave. The 150 policemen at the school tried to disperse the students and asked them to return to classes. After some of the students began fighting the police, a group of riot police arrived to try to restore order. When the police finally succeeded in quell-ing the protests, many of the students began driving through nearby streets carrying Confederate flags.

The bomb that exploded outside the Sixteenth Street Baptist Church caused the damage seen here. The explosion killed four black girls attending Sunday school. *(Courtesy of AP Images)*

A white Birmingham resident named Robert Chambliss had been responsible for the second bombing of Arthur Shores's house. He had purchased more than one hundred sticks of dynamite on September 4, and only used one and a half in his attack against Shore. This was not the first time Chambliss had taken part in violence against African Americans. In fact, he had even been given the nickname "Dynamite Bob" because of his involvement with violence planned by the Ku Klux Klan.

On the night of Saturday, September 14, Chambliss left his wife at home and went with friends from the Klan to carry out another attack. He, Bobby Cherry, and two other

Klan members planted nineteen sticks of dynamite and a timing device outside the Sixteenth Street Baptist Church. Just before 10:30 the next morning, the bomb exploded and killed four girls.

Three of the girls, Cynthia Wesley, Carole Robertson, and Addie Mae Collins, were fourteen years old; Denise McNair was just eleven. They were at the church for Sunday school and were in the basement when the bomb went off, not far from where the dynamite had been hidden outside. As church members searched through the debris, they came across the girls' bodies. The explosion blew holes in the basement, causing extensive damage to the church. More than twenty other churchgoers were also injured.

Police soon arrived, and so did a large crowd of angry African Americans. The bystanders began hurling rocks and bottles at the police and at whites who passed by in cars. Before the crowd was cleared, six more people, five of them white and one black, had been injured. On the same afternoon, two white sixteen-year-old boys shot and killed a thirteen-year-old black boy as they passed him on a scooter, apparently for no reason. Another black teenager, Johnnie Robinson, was shot in the back by police while running away after throwing rocks at a car. He was already dead by the time he was taken to a local hospital.

Martin Luther King returned to Birmingham on Sunday night, saying that he would urge the black community not to respond with violence despite the tragedy. But he also warned that if the federal government did not reassure African Americans that they would be protected, Birmingham might soon be the scene of a "racial holocaust." In a telegram to Governor Wallace, King wrote that "the blood of four little children and others critically injured is on your hands."

The FBI quickly sent twenty-five agents to Birmingham to begin an investigation of the crime. President Kennedy issued a statement expressing his sorrow over the bombing. Other political leaders from across the country condemned the killings, and papers brought the news to Americans everywhere.

While some African Americans in Birmingham grew angrier and feared that nothing would ever change, many in the white community condemned the bombing. But the guilt of most white residents only went so far. When one local businessman, Charles Morgan Jr., criticized the city's white business leaders for not doing enough to prevent racial violence, he was driven out of town by furious whites who harassed him for his speech. The local police department did little to try to solve the crime, and actually made it more difficult for the FBI to carry out its investigation. Some members of the police force had close ties to the Klan and were not likely to help convict their friends. In fact, the FBI was unable to indict anyone for the crime, and it would not be until 1977 that anyone was convicted for the bombing. That year, Robert Chambliss was finally found guilty and sentenced to life in prison. He died in jail in 1985. Decades later, in 2000, the FBI arrested two more suspects after reopening the case, Bobby Frank Cherry and Thomas Blanton. Both were found guilty and also sentenced to life in prison.

Although the summer of 1963 ended in tragedy in Birmingham, the efforts of the black community to fight for equality were not in vain. The civil rights demonstrations in April and May convinced President Kennedy that

the country needed a new civil rights bill to end legal segregation. A civil rights bill had passed in 1957, but southern
congressmen were able to prevent it from having any strong
enforcement measures. That law had done little to end discrimination in the South, but there was hope that the new
bill would have more success.

In November 1963, President Kennedy was assassinated
in Dallas, Texas. Vice President Lyndon B. Johnson assumed
the presidency and soon picked up Kennedy's call for a strong
civil rights bill. In July 1964, the Civil Rights Act was passed
and signed by Johnson. It made discrimination in employment
illegal and banned segregation in stores, hotels, and all other
public facilities. The next year, Congress passed the Voting
Rights Act, which made it illegal for states to use poll taxes
or other qualifications to limit voter registration. After the act
passed, thousands of African Americans in the South were
able to register to vote for the first time. These new laws did
not end discrimination, but they did go a long way toward
establishing greater equality for all Americans.

The victories of the civil rights movement, particularly
the Civil Rights Act and Voting Rights Act, gave millions of
African Americans opportunities that would not have been
possible without the courage of those who had been willing
to face fire hoses and police dogs to stand up for their rights.
Before the spring of 1963, Birmingham seemed an unlikely
place for the civil rights movement to achieve one of its most
important victories. By the end of that long summer, the city
of Birmingham would forever be linked to the struggle for
equality and justice.

Timeline

1954   Supreme Court rules in *Brown v. Board of Education of Topeka, Kansas* that "separate but equal" schools are unconstitutional.

1955   Rosa Parks arrested in Montgomery, Alabama, after refusing to give up seat on bus to white man; Montgomery Bus Boycott starts a few days later, leads to a Supreme Court ruling declaring segregation on city buses unconstitutional.

1956   Fred Shuttlesworth helps create Alabama Christian Movement for Human Rights in Birmingham, Alabama.

1957   Martin Luther King Jr., and other ministers form the Southern Christian Leadership Conference.

1960   Four college students in Greensboro, North Carolina, sit in at a lunch counter and trigger a wave of sit-ins across the South.

1961		Freedom Riders leave Washington, D.C.; riders attacked at Birmingham bus station when they arrive on May 14.
1962		Birmingham voters choose to change form of city government.
1963	**April 2**	Albert Boutwell elected new mayor of Birmingham.
	April 3	Civil rights campaign begins.
	April 12	Martin Luther King Jr., goes to jail.
	May 2	Students begin taking part in the demonstrations.
	May 10	Agreement reached, ending the protests.
	Aug. 28	More than 200,000 people gather for the March on Washington, where King gives his famous "I Have a Dream" speech.
	Sept. 15	Members of the Ku Klux Klan set off a bomb at the Sixteenth Street Baptist Church, killing four girls.
1964		Congress passes Civil Rights Act.
1965		Congress passes Voting Rights Act.

Sources

CHAPTER ONE: Birmingham Jail

p. 13, "Birmingham is probably . . . is widely known," James
M. Washington, ed., *Testament of Hope: The
Essential Writings and Speeches of Martin Luther King
Jr.* (San Francisco: Harpers San Francisco, 1986), 292.

p. 13, "We had no alternative . . ." Ibid.

p. 14, "moral responsibility to disobey . . ." Ibid.

p. 14, "For years now, I . . ." Ibid.

CHAPTER TWO: The Magic City

p. 25, "disorders and bloodshed and . . ." Glenn Eskew,
But For Birmingham (Chapel Hill: University of
North Carolina Press, 1997) 62.

p. 25, "Negro citizens are bottled . . ." Ibid., 63.

p. 26, "I believed in them . . ." Lewis W. Jones, "Fred
L. Shuttlesworth: Indigenous Leader," *Birmingham, Alabama,
1956-1963: The Black Struggle for Civil Rights,*
(Brooklyn, NY: Carlson, 1989), 118.

p. 27, "I would rather hear . . ." Ibid.

CHAPTER THREE: The Freedom Rides Come to Birmingham

p. 36, "One passenger was knocked . . ." "Bi-Racial

Buses Attacked, Riders Beaten in Alabama," *New York Times,* May 16, 1961.

CHAPTER FIVE: Struggling Toward Civil Rights

p. 51, "The patience of an oppressed . . ." Marjorie White, *A Walk To Freedom: The Reverend Fred Shuttlesworth and the Alabama Christian Movement For Human Rights, 1956-1964* (Birmingham: Birmingham Historical Society, 1998),

p. 56, "We can not in . . ." Eskew, *But For Birmingham*, 238.

CHAPTER SIX: Keeping the Campaign Alive

p. 58, "injustice anywhere is a . . ." Washington, *Testament of Hope,* 292.

p. 58-59, "You may well ask . . ." Ibid.

p. 60, "Oppressed people cannot remain . . ." Ibid.

p. 60, "the Negro has many . . ." David J. Garrow, *Bearing the Cross: Martin Luther King, Jr., and the Southern Christian Leadership Conference* (New York: William Morrow, 1986), 237.

p. 61, "Whatever our shortcomings . . ." "New Birmingham Regime Sworn, Raising Hopes for Racial Peace," *New York Times*, April 16, 1963.

CHAPTER SEVEN: Saved by the Students

p. 67, "I have been inspired and . . ." Eskew, *But For Birmingham*, 265.

p. 69, "They've turned the fire . . ." Taylor Branch, *Parting the Waters: America in the King Years, 1954-63* (New York: Simon and Schuster, 1988), 759.

p. 69, "If the white power structure . . ." "Dogs and Hoses Repulse Negroes at Birmingham," *New York Times*, May 4, 1963.

p. 70, "Continued refusal to grant . . . afford to pay," "Robert Kennedy Warns of Increasing Turmoil," *New York Times*, May 4, 1963.

p. 72, "Turn on your . . ." Branch, *Parting the Waters*, 767.

p. 73, "If we can crack . . ." "Birmingham Talks Pushed; Negroes March Peacefully," *New York Times*, May 6, 1963.

p. 73, "left-wing," "Wallace Says Birmingham Is 'Fed Up' With Protests," *New York Times*, May 6, 1963.

CHAPTER EIGHT: An Uneasy Truce

p. 75, "Join the thousand in . . ." "Waves of Chanting Students Seized—Talks Bog Down," *New York Times*, May 7, 1963.

p. 79, "I wish they'd carried . . ." "Rioting Negroes Routed by Police at Birmingham," *New York Times*, May 8, 1963.

p. 79, "open defiance of uniformed . . ." "Birmingham Paper's Plea to Kennedy," *New York Times*, May 8, 1963.

p. 82, "look forward now to . . ." "Birmingham Pact Sets Timetable for Integration," *New York Times*, May 11, 1963.

p. 82, "I'm unwilling to make . . . agitators out of town," "Birmingham Talks Reach an Accord on Ending Crisis," *New York Times*, May 10, 1963.

CHAPTER NINE: Backlash

p. 85, "Our home was just . . ." Branch, *Parting the Waters*, 795.

p. 86, "I do not feel... law of the land," "50 Hurt in Negro Rioting After Birmingham Blasts," *New York Times*, May 13, 1963.

p. 86, "would use all available . . . " "President John F. Kennedy: The President's News Conference, May 8,

1963," the American Presidency Project, Web site of John Woolley and Gerhard Peters at the University of California, Santa Barbara, http://www.presidency.ucsb.edu/ws/index.php?pid=9192

p. 86, "the local leaders . . ." Ibid.

p. 88, "I'm sorry, but I . . ." Ibid., 802.

p. 90-91, "Now is the time . . ." Washington, *Testament of Hope,* 292.

p. 91, "I have a dream . . ." Ibid.

CHAPTER TEN: The Legacy of Birmingham

p. 95, "Go home . . ." "Wallace Ends Resistance As Guard Is Federalized," *New York Times*, September 11, 1963.

p. 97-98, "Racial holocaust . . . on your hands," "Dr. King goes to Birmingham," *New York Times*, September 16, 1963.

Bibliography

Adams, Francis D., and Barry Sanders. *Alienable Rights: The Exclusion of African Americans in a White Man's Land, 1619-2000.* New York: Perennial, 2003.

"Birmingham Pact Sets Timetable for Integration." *New York Times,* May 11, 1963.

"Birmingham Paper's Plea to Kennedy." *New York Times,* May 8, 1963.

"Birmingham Talks Pushed; Negroes March Peacefully." *New York Times,* May 6, 1963.

"Birmingham Talks Reach an Accord on Ending Crisis." *New York Times,* May 10, 1963

"Bi-Racial Buses Attacked, Riders Beaten in Alabama." *New York Times,* May 16, 1961.

Boyd, Herb. *We Shall Overcome.* Naperville, IL: Sourcebooks Media Fusion, 2004.

Branch, Taylor. *Parting the Waters: America in the King Years, 1954-63.* New York: Simon and Schuster, 1988.

Davis, Ronald L.F. "Creating Jim Crow: In-Depth Essay." *The History of Jim Crow.* http://www.jimcrowhistory.org.

"Dogs and Hoses Repulse Negroes at Birmingham." *New York Times,* May 4, 1963.

"Dr. King goes to Birmingham." *New York Times,* September 16, 1963.

Eskew, Glenn T. *But for Birmingham: The Local and*

National Movements in the Civil Rights Struggle.
Chapel Hill, NC: University of North Carolina
Press, 1997.

"50 Hurt in Negro Rioting After Birmingham Blasts."
New York Times, May 13, 1963.

Garrow, David J. *Bearing the Cross: Martin Luther King, Jr.,
and the Southern Christian Leadership Conference.*
New York: William Morrow, 1986.

_____. *Birmingham, Alabama, 1956-1963: The Black
Struggle for Civil Rights. Vol. 8 of Martin Luther
King, Jr., and the Civil Rights Movement.* Brooklyn,
NY: Carlson, 1989.

King, Martin Luther, Jr. *A Testament of Hope: The Essential
Writings and Speeches of Martin Luther King Jr.* Edited
by James M. Washington. San Francisco: Harpers
San Francisco, 1986.

McWhorter, Diane. *Carry Me Home: Birmingham, Alabama,
The Climactic Battle of the Civil Rights Revolution.*
New York: Simon & Schuster, 2001.

Miller, William Robert. *Martin Luther King, Jr: His
Life, Martyrdom and Meaning for the World.* New
York: Weybright and Talley, 1968.

"New Birmingham Regime Sworn, Raising Hopes for
Racial Peace." *New York Times*, April 16, 1963.

Reddick, L.D. *Crusader Without Violence: A Biography of
Martin Luther King, Jr.* New York: Harper &
Brothers, 1959.

"Rioting Negroes Routed by Police at Birmingham." *New
York Times*, May 8, 1963.

"Robert Kennedy Warns of Increasing Turmoil." *New
York Times*, May 4, 1963.

"Wallace Ends Resistance As guard Is Federalized." *New
York Times*, September 11, 1963.

"Wallace Says Birmingham Is 'Fed Up' With Protests."
  New York Times, May 6, 1963.
"Waves of Chanting Students Seized—Talks Bog Down."
  New York Times, May 7, 1963.

Web sites

http://www.pbs.org/wgbh/amex/eyesontheprize/story/07_c.html
Inside this PBS Web site, learn about "Project 'C'" in Birmingham. There's information on Birmingham organizer Rev. Fred Shuttlesworth, a telegram from Governor George Wallace to President John F. Kennedy warning Kennedy not to send federal troops to Birmingham, and a collection of photos, among other features.

http://www.english.uiuc.edu/maps/poets/m_r/randall/birmingham.htm
Modern American Poetry, a Web site hosted by the Department of English at the University of Illinois at Urbana-Champaign, features a page on "Birmingham, Alabama, and the Civil Rights Movement in 1963." The page is a collection of news stories and magazine articles, along with profiles of the four girls killed in the Sixteenth Street Baptist Church bombing, Martin Luther King's eulogy for the young victims, the lyrics to Richard Farina's 1964 song "Birmingham Sunday," and a legal chronology of the bombing case.

Index

Sixteenth Street Baptist Church as it looks today. *(Courtesy of AP Images)*